ALL ABOUT ME

My name is ....

I am .... years old

My favourite colour is ....

HOW TO USE THIS BOOK

This book has been made with a growing brain in mind!

The good news is it's fun and there is no right or wrong way to fill in your Doodle Diary.

All we ask is for you to try and be super honest and true to yourself!

It's important you speak to an adult you trust if there is something really worrying you. Even us adults need help from others when things get tricky!

Let your imagination run wild and escape into your own world through this creative journal.

Being playful can be a great way to explore things in your mind and see them from the outside.

You are you and that's amazing! Remember, you are writing your own story, not anyone else's.

This is a safe place that is yours and only yours. Show your awesomeness through creativity!

OUR TOP TIPS

BE BRAVE!

Find the courage to try new things, you never know how it might turn out! Even great artists doodled their visions and some even became famous painters by starting with just a few scribbles!

USE DIFFERENT SHAPES

You can create almost anything from a series of shapes!

MAKE PATTERNS BY REPETITION

Try using the same shape over and over to make your very own pattern design.

GET SQUIGGLY BY LETTING YOUR PENCIL GO WILD ON THE PAGE

Don't forget we all have to start somewhere so just see where your art takes you!

BE BOLD

Use lots of colour to decorate your page!

Be inspired by nature

There are amazing things all around you! Look for shapes in the natural world to explore your creative flair.

Get cutting and sticking

You can also use collage to create awesome pictures. Just cut out things that interest you from old magazines or newspapers to create texture and add interest to your journal.

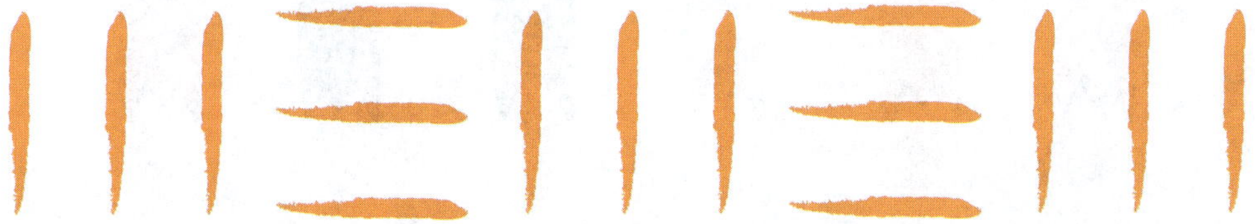

Look how Fox repeats lines over and over again to make a pattern!

THE POSITIVE PENCILS

Together they make the team!

The Positive Pencils have created this journal for you to explore your feelings and build confidence through writing and creativity!

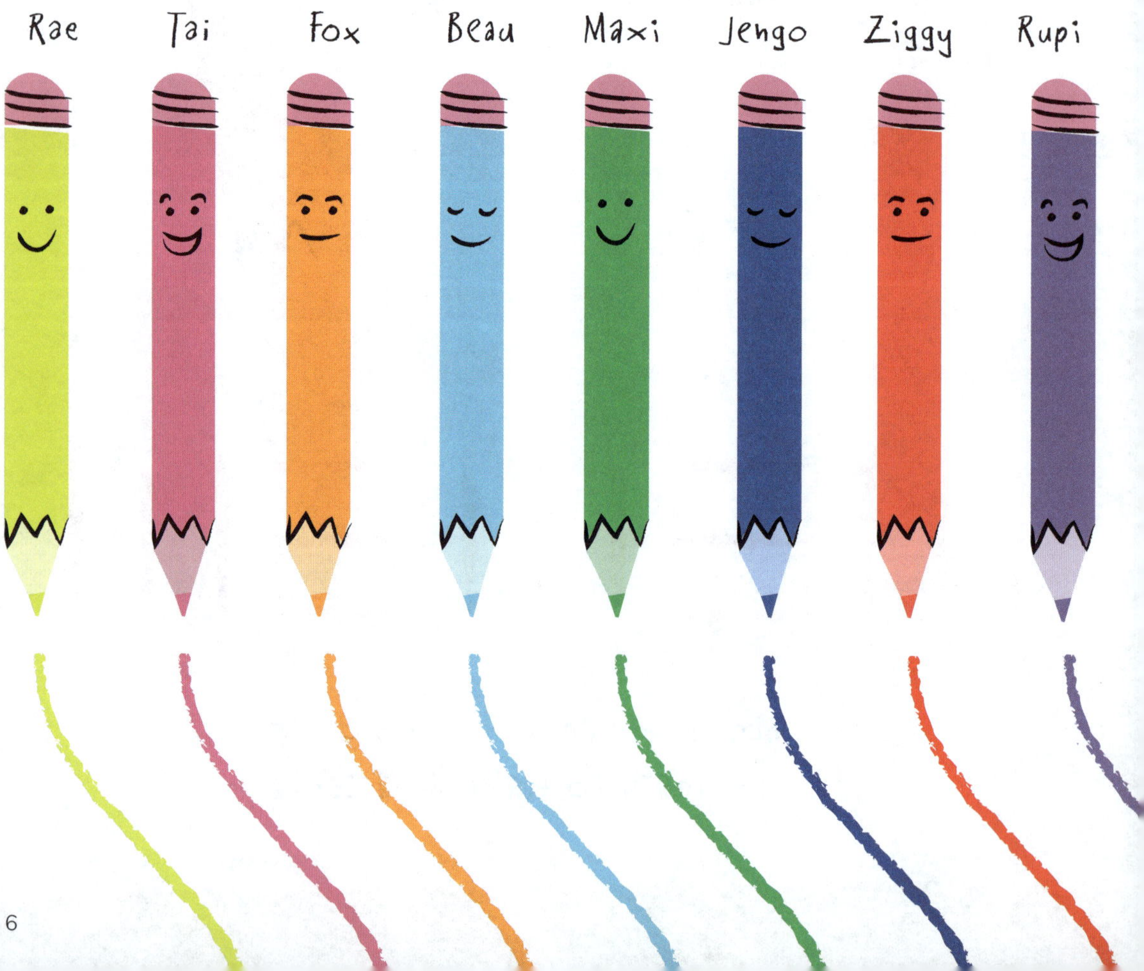

TOGETHER WE MAKE THE

WORLD A BRIGHTER PLACE

AN EXAMPLE

DEAR DIARY

Date: 2 / 3 /25 Day: friday

Choose your weather mood

Dear diary...

Today was quite a good day! I was in a happy mood as it's nearly the weekend!

What would I like to remember about today?

- We did 'relaxtime' on the carp
- I played with Orla at lunchti
- we went to the swings

Today I took care of myself by:

I ate all of my lunch and I drank ALL my water bottl

Today I am grateful for:

My cat Jasper. He always ma me feel calm on the sofa

MY DOODLE DIARY
no
rain,
no
flowers

WEATHER MOODS

It's important to track your moods to see what you have been feeling.

We have given you these weather symbols so you can choose your mood each day...

Our feelings key:

You can choose as many as you like in one day!

YOUR MOOD PENCIL

Use colour to express your feelings.

You'll find a blank pencil on each of your doodle pages.

Use the colours of the weather to express how you have felt throughout the day.

For example...

This morning I felt calm

Then I felt happy

Then I felt worried

Remember there is NO right and wrong way to use this journal, these are all just suggestions!

I CAN TAP INTO MY EMOTIONS

FEELINGS AREN'T GOOD OR BAD

Some feelings we experience may be a bit unpleasant but there is no right or wrong feeling. We want to help you make sense of these feelings and work out what you may need in order to move forward!

Understanding what our feelings are trying to tell us is the most important thing and something even us adults need to work on!

Feelings are like the weather, always changing!

BODIES

We all have a **MENTAL HEALTH** and a **PHYSICAL HEALTH**

Our mental health is linked to our brain

Our physical health is linked to the rest of our body

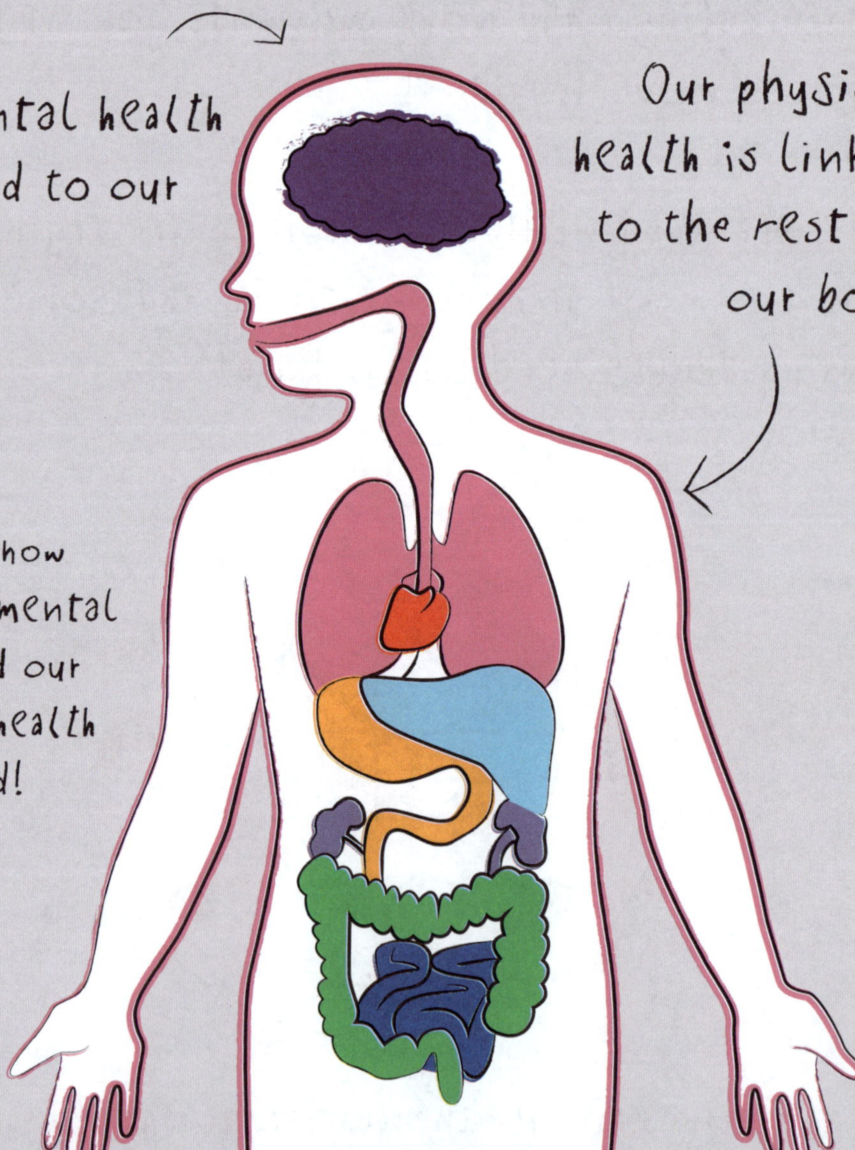

We now know that our mental health and our physical health are linked!

Feelings in my mind and body

Our brains are so awesome, think of them like mission control!

We have feelings that are physical aches and pains

but we also

have feelings that are emotional, like sadness, joy and jealousy.

FIXED MINDSET EXAMPLES

(Make us feel stuck)

GROWTH MINDSET EXAMPLES

(Help us grow)

DEAR DIARY

Date: / / Day: ____________________

Choose your weather mood

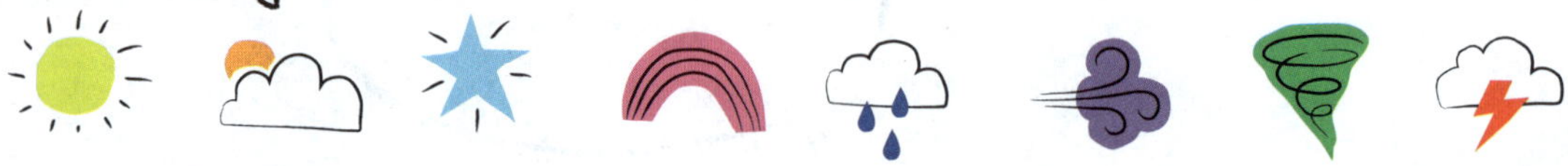

Dear diary...

....

....

....

What would I like to remember about today?

- ....
- ....
- ....

Today I took care of myself by: ....

....

....

Today I am grateful for: ....

....

....

MY DOODLE DIARY

I HAVE A GROWTH MINDSET

WHAT IS A GROWTH MINDSET?

Look at this picture and imagine it is your brain.

Which side would you like your brain to look like?

DEAR DIARY

Date: / /   Day: ____________________

Choose your weather mood

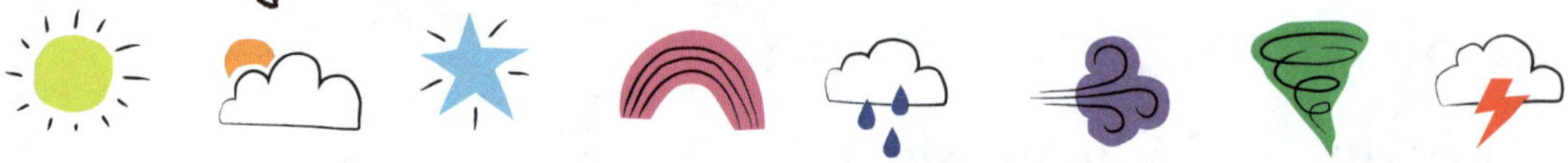

Dear diary...

....

....

....

What would I like to remember about today?

- ....
- ....
- ....

Today I took care of myself by:

....

....

Today I am grateful for:

....

....

MY DOODLE DIARY

I

CAN

FREE

MY

MIND

Visualise this...

Doodling is a great way to free up thinking space and help you work out what you need.

You can go wild and explore your imagination because there is no right or wrong! It's all about getting lost in your imagination.

Imagine what these marks could be and finish off the doodle!

DEAR DIARY

Date: / /   Day: ____________

Choose your weather mood

Dear diary...

What would I like to remember about today?

-
-
-

Today I took care of myself by:

Today I am grateful for:

MY DOODLE DIARY

I
CAN
GROUND
MYSELF

Using my senses

If you feel yourself getting into a panic, you can use this idea to help make your mind calm and grounded again.

Look around you...

Name **5** things you can **see**

Name **4** things you can **hear**

Name **3** things you can **touch**

Name **2** things you can **smell**

Name **1** thing you can **taste**

DEAR DIARY

Date: / /   Day: ______________

Choose your weather mood

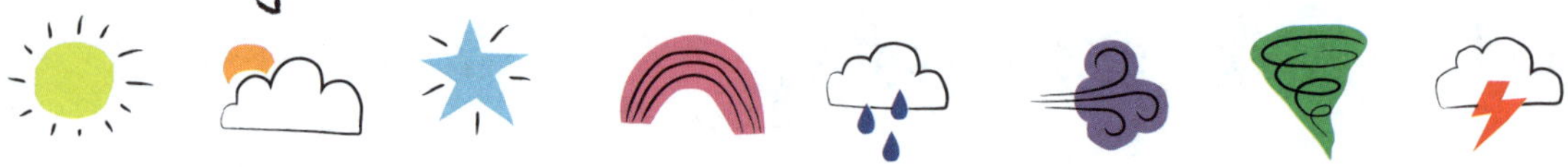

Dear diary...

What would I like to remember about today?

-
-
-

Today I took care of myself by:

Today I am grateful for:

MY DOODLE DIARY

I
CAN
FIND
POSITIVES
IN MYSELF

MIRROR MIRROR

Write or draw
all the positives
you can find in
yourself when
you look in your
'Positive Mirror'

DEAR DIARY

Date: / /

Day: ____________

Choose your weather mood

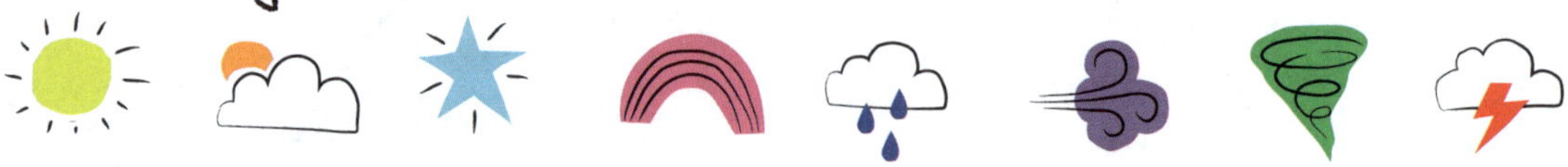

Dear diary...

What would I like to remember about today?

•

•

•

Today I took care of myself by:

Today I am grateful for:

MY DOODLE DIARY

I MAKE
TIME
FOR
THINGS
I LOVE

MY FULL HEART

Fill this jigsaw with all the things, people and places you LOVE!

DEAR DIARY

Date: / /

Day: ____________

Choose your weather mood

Dear diary...

What would I like to remember about today?

•

•

•

Today I took care of myself by:

Today I am grateful for:

MY DOODLE DIARY

I
CAN
MAKE
MY OWN
HAPPINESS

MY HAPPY JAR

Fill this jar with words and memories that make you happy

DEAR DIARY

Date: / /   Day: ____________

Choose your weather mood

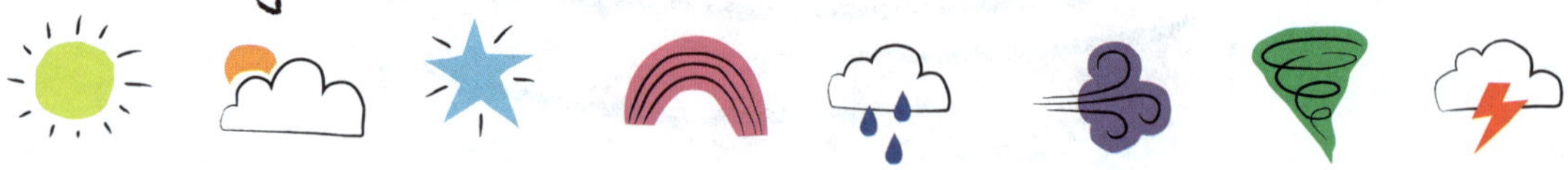

Dear diary...

What would I like to remember about today?

-
-
-

Today I took care of myself by:

Today I am grateful for:

MY DOODLE DIARY

I AM UNIQUE

10 GOOD THINGS ALL ABOUT ME...

1

2

3

4

5

6

7

8

9

10

DEAR DIARY

Date: / /

Day: ______________

Choose your weather mood

Dear diary...

What would I like to remember about today?

-
-
-

Today I took care of myself by:

Today I am grateful for:

MY DOODLE DIARY

I CAN LEARN TO LET GO

VISUALISE THIS...

Imagine you are high in the sky in a hot air balloon. Breathe in the fresh air and look around you at the world below.

Then imagine that your worries are the heavy sandbags attached to the sides of the basket.

One by one, drop them off the side and feel yourself get lighter and fly higher and higher.

DEAR DIARY

Date: / /

Day: ____________

Choose your weather mood

Dear diary...

What would I like to remember about today?

-
-
-

Today I took care of myself by:

Today I am grateful for:

MY DOODLE DIARY

UNWIND WITH BEAU

TRY YOURS HERE

We call this a BrainTangle. It helps us slow down our heart rate and calm our breathing so we can reflect on what is tangling up our minds.

DEAR DIARY

Date: / /　　　Day: ________

Choose your weather mood

Dear diary...

What would I like to remember about today?

-
-
-

Today I took care of myself by:

Today I am grateful for:

MY DOODLE DIARY

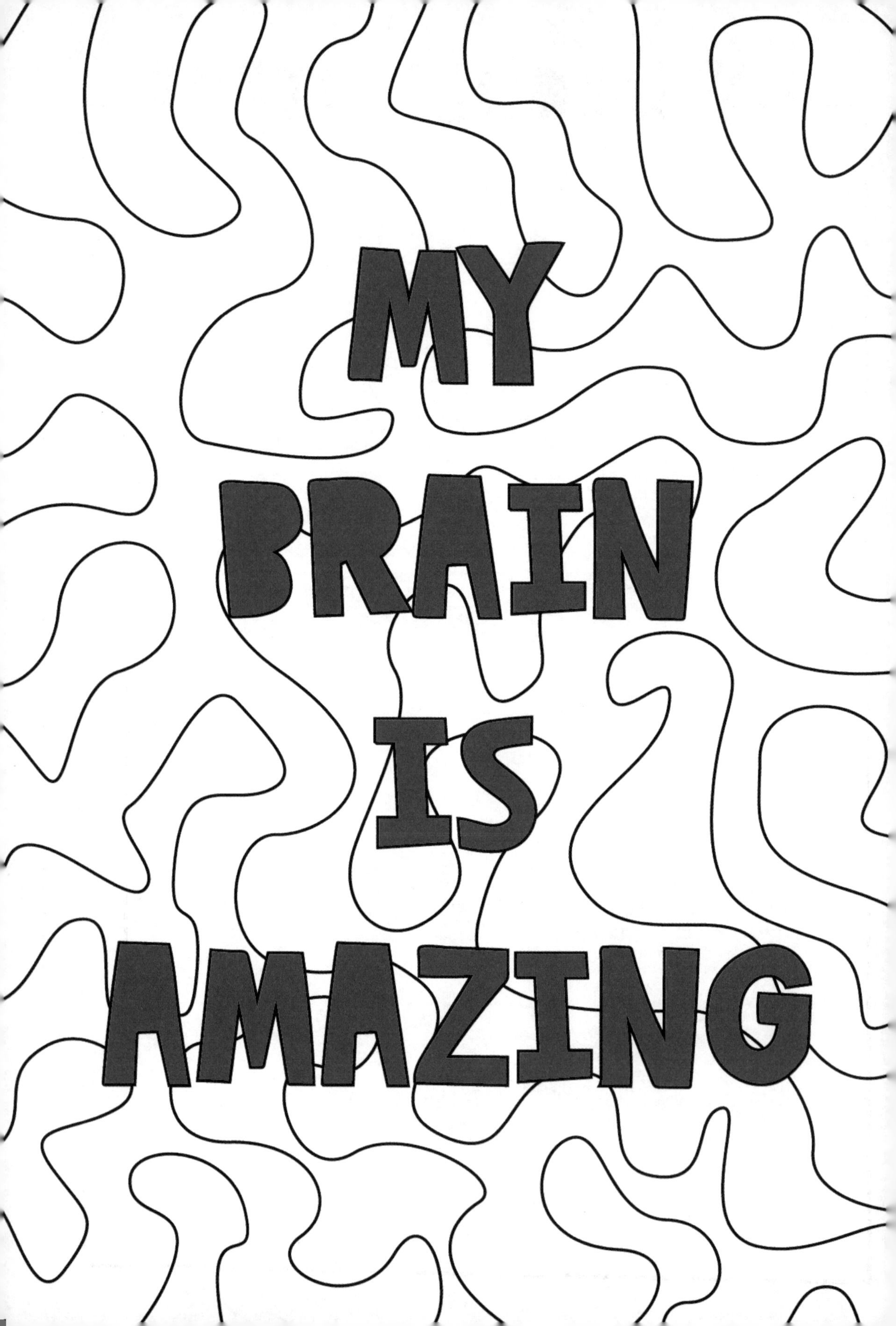
MY
BRAIN
IS
AMAZING

IT'S ALL CONNECTED!

Our brains send us messages and work hard all day long.

We need to feed our brains with lots of good stuff like water, healthy food and kind thoughts!

Every time we learn something new, a brand new connection is made...

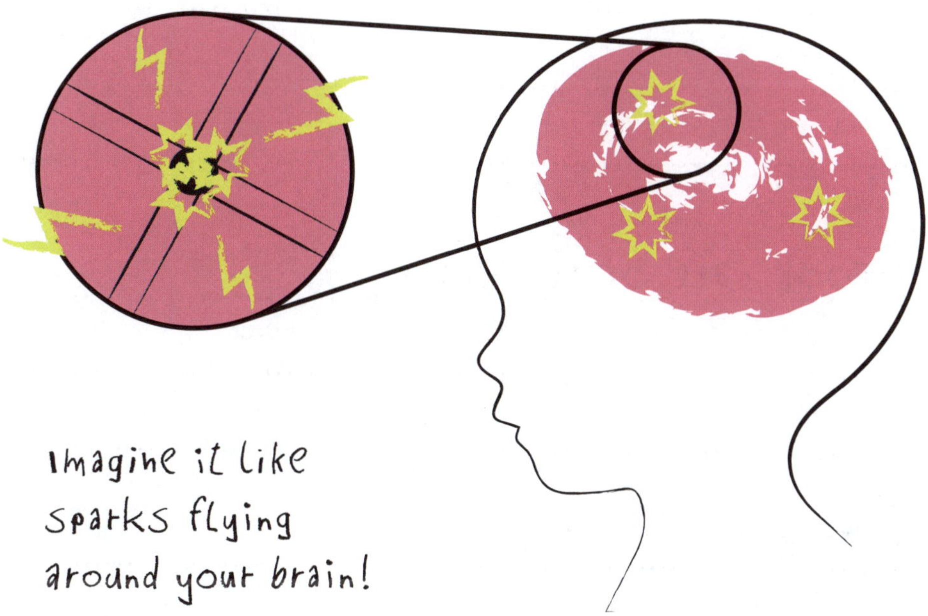

Imagine it like sparks flying around your brain!

DEAR DIARY

Date: /   /   Day: ________________

Choose your weather mood

Dear diary...

What would I like to remember about today?

-
-
-

Today I took care of myself by:

Today I am grateful for:

MY DOODLE DIARY

I
CAN
CALM
MY
MIND

WAVE DRAWING

Carry on copying these lines
to create waves...

DEAR DIARY

Date: / / Day: ____________

Choose your weather mood

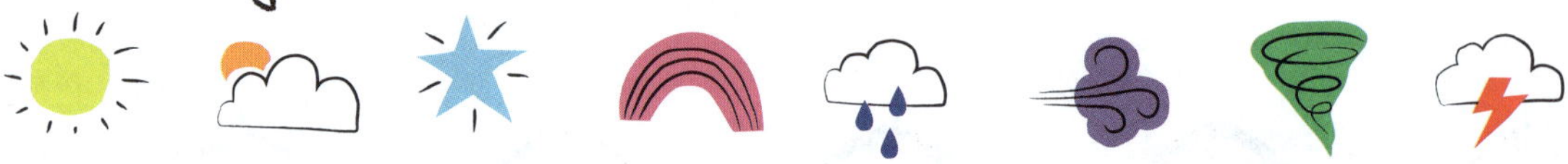

Dear diary...

What would I like to remember about today?

-
-
-

Today I took care of myself by:

Today I am grateful for:

MY DOODLE DIARY

COUNTING DOWN FROM TEN...

10

Ten

9

Nine

8

Eight

7

Seven

6

Six

Feeling overwhelmed

We can all feel like things are getting too much sometimes. Find a quiet corner and use your fingers to count backwards from 10...

1 One

2 Two

3 Three

4 Four

5 Five

DEAR DIARY

Date: / / Day: ____________

Choose your weather mood

Dear diary...

What would I like to remember about today?

-
-
-

Today I took care of myself by:

Today I am grateful for:

MY DOODLE DIARY

I AM RESILIENT

WHAT DOES IT MEAN TO BE RESILIENT?

Think of it like bouncing back like a bouncy ball.

If you experience a setback, it's okay to learn from it and try again.

It's all about getting back up again, because remember it's all about progress not perfection!

DEAR DIARY

Date: /   /   Day: ____________

Choose your weather mood

Dear diary...

What would I like to remember about today?

-
-
-

Today I took care of myself by:

Today I am grateful for:

MY DOODLE DIARY

I CAN DESCRIBE MY FEELINGS

Meet the Scribblers

The scribblers can help you explain how you are feeling. All you have to do is give them a speech bubble.

1. Do a scribble in the colour you are feeling

2. Give it eyes, hands and legs

3. Give it a voice... Use speech bubbles to say how you feel!

Try your own here!

DEAR DIARY

Date: / /

Day: ____________

Choose your weather mood

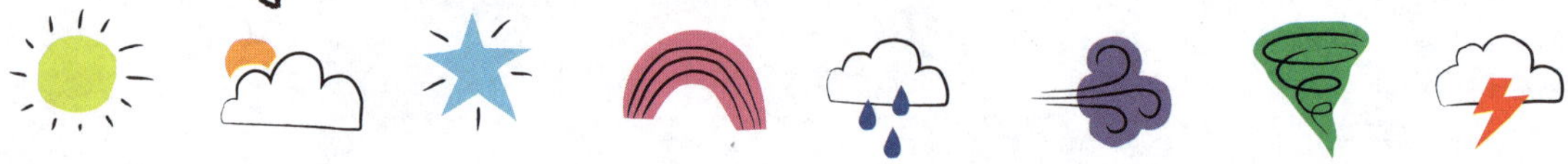

Dear diary...

What would I like to remember about today?

-
-
-

Today I took care of myself by:

Today I am grateful for:

MY DOODLE DIARY

YOGA DOO MOVING AND STRETCHING

Why do we yoga?

To keep our bodies healthy we need to try and move, stretch and take nice long deep breaths.

If we feel worried about something or want to help ourselves feel calm, trying some yoga poses helps us to relax our body and mind and feel great!

All you need is a mat or rug or even a towel. Let's get started!

LET'S GROW INTO A TREE!

We are going to learn 'Tree Pose'

Let's start by being a little seed. Make yourself as tiny as you can and close your eyes, just like you are a seed planted in the ground.

As the sun shines, you start to grow into a tree. Put your hands together and start to grow up tall towards the sunshine.

Squat as a baby tree, take a few deep breaths as you get ready to grow.

Grow taller and plant your feet on the ground, these are your roots, holding you strong in the earth.

Your arms, or branches, grow towards the sunshine and out to the side. Wiggle your fingers if you are a fruit tree. Your branches might be blowing in the wind, gently sway from side to side.

Make sure your body, the trunk, is as tall as possible. If you feel strong you could look at a point straight ahead and slowly lift up one foot and place it on the other one.

Can you slide it higher up your leg?

You're balancing!
Well done little tree!

DEAR DIARY

Date: / /   Day: ____________

Choose your weather mood

Dear diary...

....

....

....

What would I like to remember about today?

- ....
- ....
- ....

Today I took care of myself by: ....

....

....

Today I am grateful for: ....

....

....

MY DOODLE DIARY

I
LEARN
FROM
MY
MISTAKES

MAXI THE MISTAKE MASTER

When Maxi makes a mistake it doesn't matter, Maxi knows there's learning to be had from it!

My name ~~iz~~ is Maxi!

Maxi simply recognises the mistake, puts a line through it and moves on!

DEAR DIARY

Date: / / Day: ______________

Choose your weather mood

Dear diary...

What would I like to remember about today?

-
-
-

Today I took care of myself by:

Today I am grateful for:

MY DOODLE DIARY

HAVE
COURAGE
AND
BE
KIND

TIMES WHEN I WAS BRAVE

Write or draw them here!

DEAR DIARY

Date: /   /   Day: ______________

Choose your weather mood

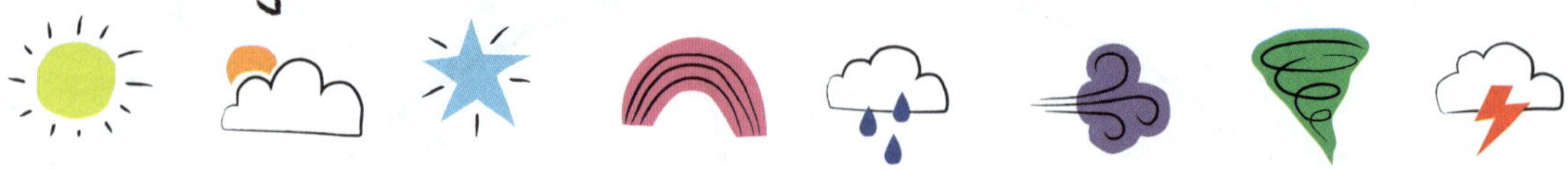

Dear diary...

What would I like to remember about today?

-
-
-

Today I took care of myself by:

Today I am grateful for:

MY DOODLE DIARY

WE ALL HAVE DIFFERENT STRENGTHS

5 THINGS THAT MAKE ME, ME!

We are all different. Can you list five things that make you great?

★

★

★

★

★

DEAR DIARY

Date: / / Day: ____________

Choose your weather mood

Dear diary...

What would I like to remember about today?

-
-
-

Today I took care of myself by:

Today I am grateful for:

MY DOODLE DIARY

I MAY BE SMALL, BUT I AM MIGHTY

WE ARE ALL SUPERHEROES

My superpower is ______________________

Design your own cape!

DEAR DIARY

Date: /   /   Day: ______________

Choose your weather mood

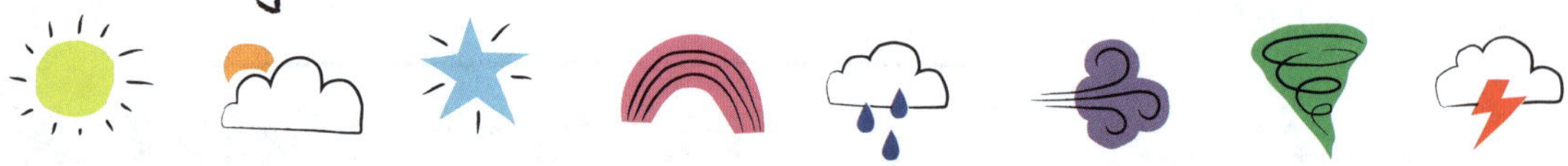

Dear diary...

What would I like to remember about today?

-
-
-

Today I took care of myself by:

Today I am grateful for:

MY DOODLE DIARY

I CAN ALWAYS USE MY BREATH

BLOW AWAY THE WORRY CLOUDS

Imagine your worries are clouds in the sky, take a deep breath and blow them away.

Imagine them floating away, getting smaller and smaller until they are finally gone!

DEAR DIARY

Date: / /   Day: ____________

Choose your weather mood

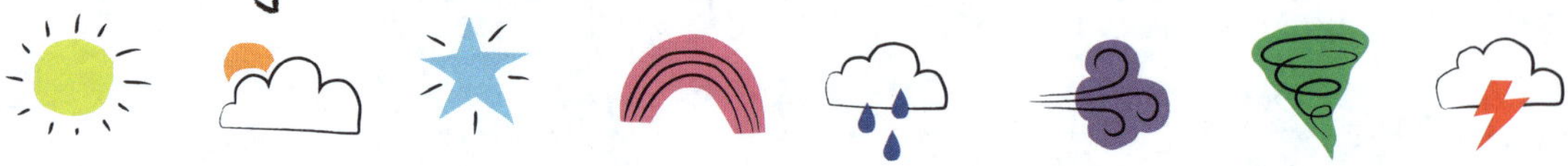

Dear diary...

What would I like to remember about today?

-
-
-

Today I took care of myself by:

Today I am grateful for:

MY DOODLE DIARY

I WILL TALK TO MYSELF AS I WOULD A FRIEND

BE KIND

Sometimes our thoughts can be unkind to us. But a good thing to do is ask yourself... "Would a friend say that to me?"

Try and write some kind things that a friend might say to you...

DEAR DIARY

Date: / /

Day: ________________

Choose your weather mood

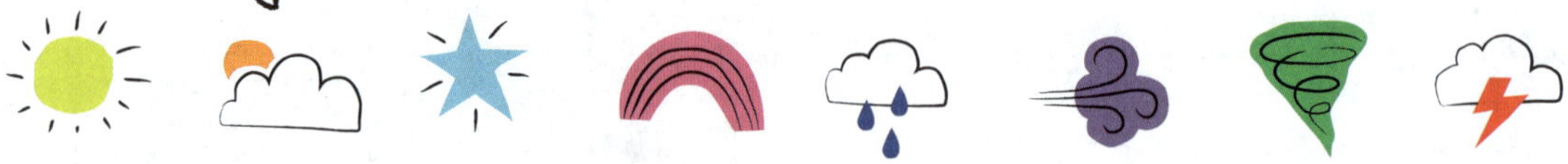

Dear diary...

What would I like to remember about today?

-
-
-

Today I took care of myself by:

Today I am grateful for:

MY DOODLE DIARY

I
AM
LOVED

REASONS PEOPLE LOVE ME

DEAR DIARY

Date: / /

Day: ______________

Choose your weather mood

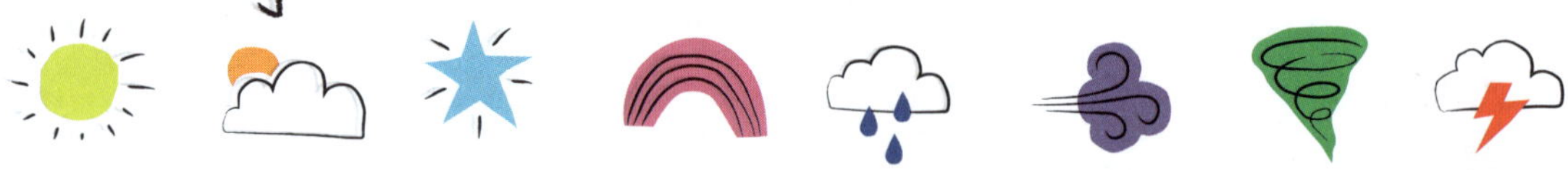

Dear diary...

What would I like to remember about today?

-
-
-

Today I took care of myself by:

Today I am grateful for:

MY DOODLE DIARY

I
BELIEVE
IN MY
OWN
ABILITY

CLIMBING A MOUNTAIN

Rupi is preparing to go on a journey.

Do you think it will be easier to go up the side or...

...break it down into chunks and tackle the mountain step-by-step?

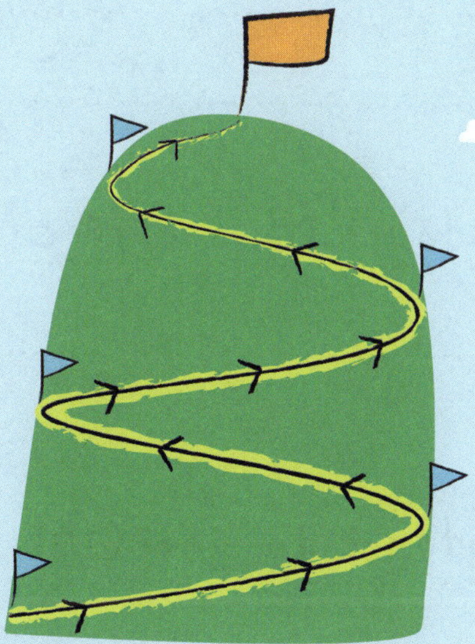

DEAR DIARY

Date: / / Day: ____________

Choose your weather mood

Dear diary...

What would I like to remember about today?

-
-
-

Today I took care of myself by:

Today I am grateful for:

MY DOODLE DIARY

I

CAN

AND

I

WILL

YOU CAN DO IT!

Draw or write about a time when you didn't think you could, but you did!

DEAR DIARY

Date: / / Day: ____________

Choose your weather mood

Dear diary...

What would I like to remember about today?

•

•

•

Today I took care of myself by:

Today I am grateful for:

MY DOODLE DIARY

I

CAN

DO

HARD

THINGS

HARD THINGS GET EASIER WITH PRACTICE

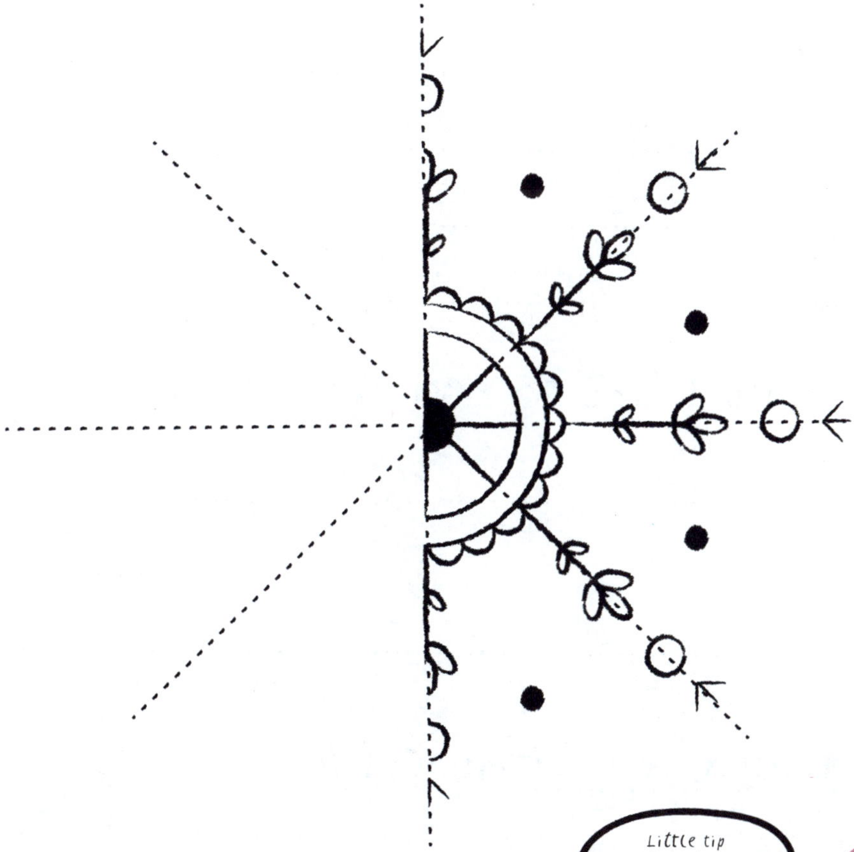

See if you can concentrate very hard and copy this pattern exactly so that it is symmetrical.

DEAR DIARY

Date: / / Day: ____________

Choose your weather mood

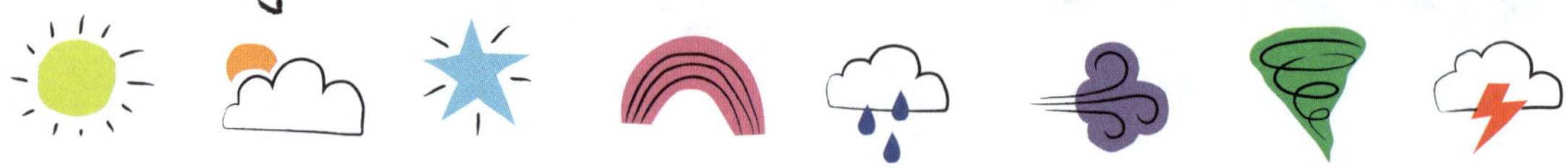

Dear diary...

What would I like to remember about today?

-
-
-

Today I took care of myself by:

Today I am grateful for:

MY DOODLE DIARY

WHAT DOES GRATITUDE MEAN?

Being grateful is feeling thankful for things in our life that make us feel happy.

THINGS I AM GRATEFUL FOR

List all the things that you are grateful for in the sun's rays. Let your gratitude sun warm you up!

DEAR DIARY

Date: / / Day: ____________

Choose your weather mood

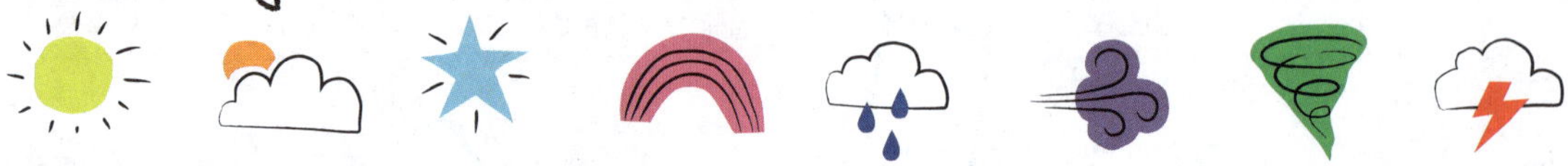

Dear diary...

What would I like to remember about today?

-
-
-

Today I took care of myself by:

Today I am grateful for:

MY DOODLE DIARY

I CAN USE MY IMAGINATION

MY PERFECT DAY LOOKS LIKE...

Morning...

Lunch...

Afternoon...

Evening...

DEAR DIARY

Date: /   /   Day: ____________

Choose your weather mood

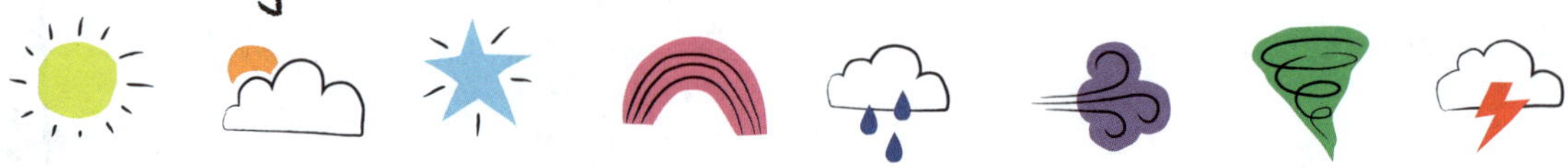

Dear diary...

What would I like to remember about today?

-
-
-

Today I took care of myself by:

Today I am grateful for:

MY DOODLE DIARY

DREAMS
DON'T
WORK
UNLESS
YOU DO

DREAM BIG

Write or draw your hopes and dreams for the future...

DEAR DIARY

Date: / / Day: ____________

Choose your weather mood

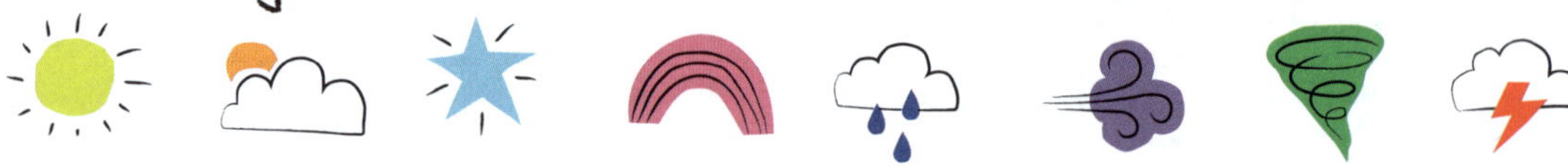

Dear diary...

What would I like to remember about today?

-
-
-

Today I took care of myself by:

Today I am grateful for:

MY DOODLE DIARY

I CAN'T CONTROL ANYONE ELSE BUT I CAN CONTROL MYSELF

CIRCLE OF CONTROL

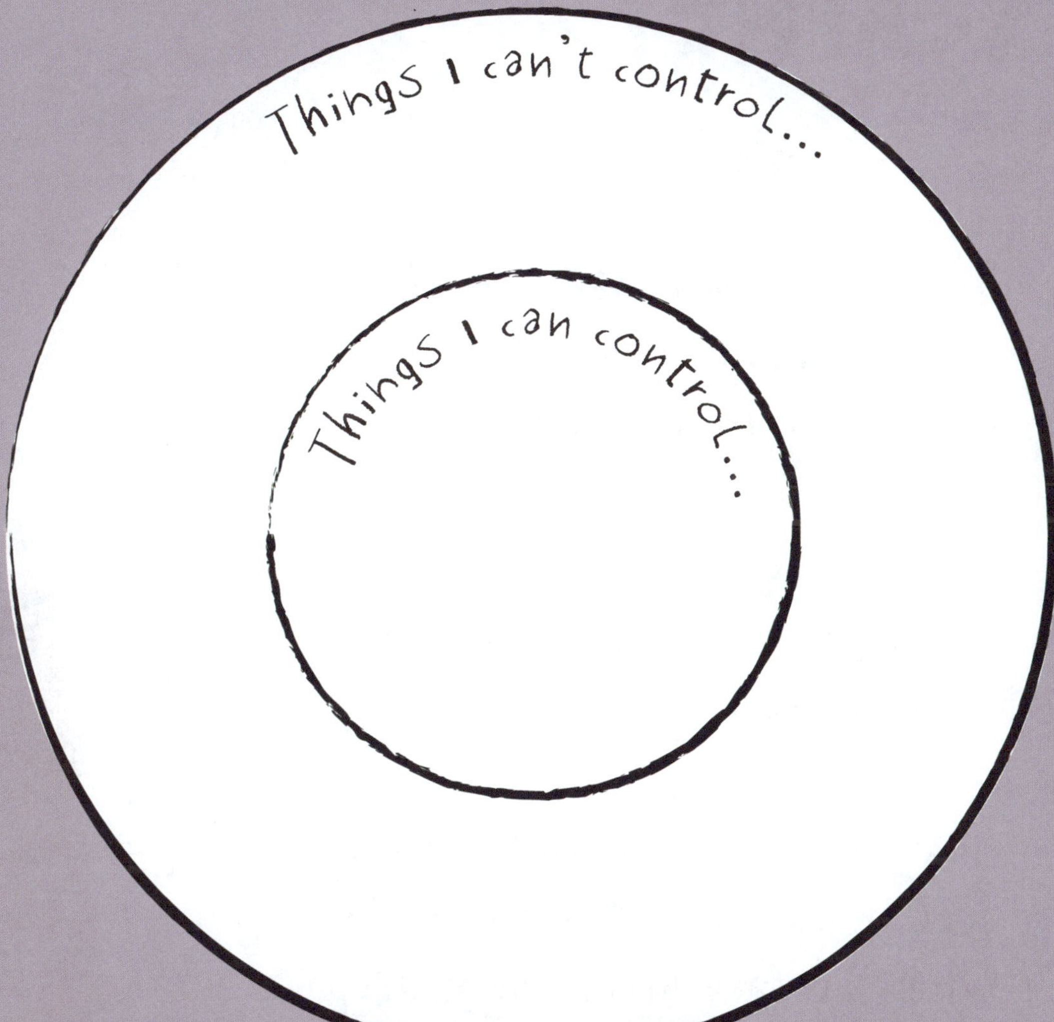

Write in the inner circle examples of things you **CAN CONTROL**, like 'my behaviour'.

Then in the outer circle write things that you **CAN'T CONTROL**, like 'my friend's reaction'.

WHY DO WE BREATHE?

Did you know humans breathe around 20,000 times a day?! How many do you notice?

We breathe air in and out through our nose and mouth into our lungs.

How we breathe changes how we feel in our body and our mind. When we take nice, long, deep breaths it helps us feel calmer and more relaxed.

Why not take a deep breath right now?

LET'S MEDITATE

Ocean Wave Breath

We are standing on the edge of the seashore, let's use the waves to help us feel calm.

Close your eyes, let's see if we can hear the sea.

Breathe in and out through your nose.

Breathe in, the wave is sucked back to the ocean.

Breathe out, the waves roll towards your toes.

Feel calm as you breathe like the waves.

DEAR DIARY

Date: / / Day:

Choose your weather mood

Dear diary...

What would I like to remember about today?

-
-
-

Today I took care of myself by:

Today I am grateful for:

MY DOODLE DIARY

RAINY
DAYS CAN
BRING
RAINBOWS

DARK
SKIES
BRING
STARS TO
SHINE

DEAR DIARY

Date: / /

Day: ________________

Choose your weather mood

Dear diary...

What would I like to remember about today?

-
-
-

Today I took care of myself by:

Today I am grateful for:

MY DOODLE DIARY

T

H

I

N

K

USE YOUR BRAIN

It's good to get used to asking yourself questions.

Use the word '**THINK**' to be more curious...

T - Is it true?

H - Is it helpful?

I - Is it inspiring?

N - Is it necessary?

K - Is it kind?

DEAR DIARY

Date: / / Day: ______________

Choose your weather mood

Dear diary...

What would I like to remember about today?

-
-
-

Today I took care of myself by:

Today I am grateful for:

MY DOODLE DIARY

I

CAN

WRITE

DOWN MY

WORRIES

THE WORRY BIN

This is the worry bin, you can imagine yourself throwing all your worries in this bin.

If you like, you can actually try writing down your worries on a piece of paper and then scrunching it up and throwing it in a real bin!

DEAR DIARY

Date: / / Day: ________________

Choose your weather mood

Dear diary...

What would I like to remember about today?

-
-
-

Today I took care of myself by:

Today I am grateful for:

MY DOODLE DIARY

IT'S OK
TO MAKE
MISTAKES

STRENGTH OF MIND

Did you know that when we make mistakes we actually help our brains to grow?

Repeat after me...
"My brain is a muscle and making mistakes is like lifting weights."

DEAR DIARY

Date: / /

Day:

Choose your weather mood

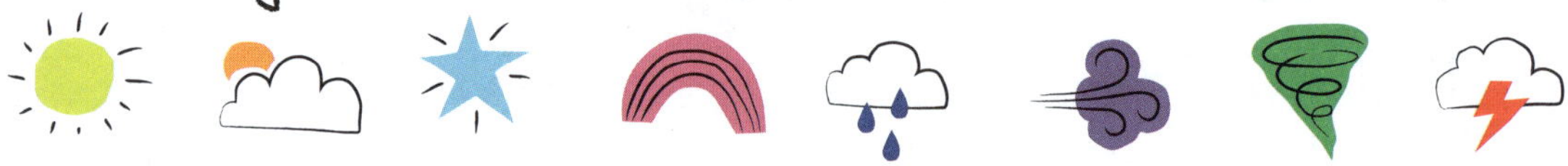

Dear diary...

What would I like to remember about today?

-
-
-

Today I took care of myself by:

Today I am grateful for:

MY DOODLE DIARY

KEEP ON
SWIMMING

Keep on keeping on

Sometimes we have to be strong and keep going even though it is hard for us.

Think of yourself like a fish swimming upstream, it's tough going but you've got this!

DEAR DIARY

Date: / /   Day: ____________

Choose your weather mood

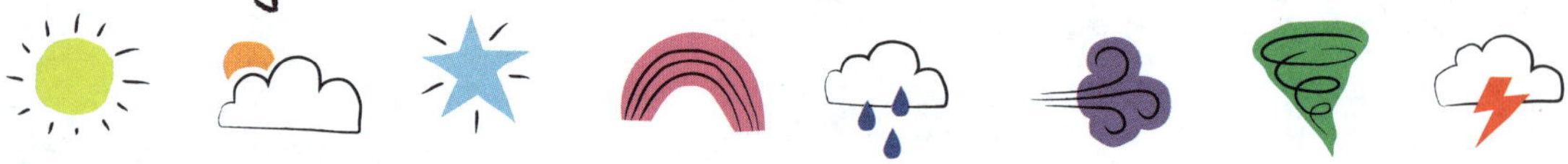

Dear diary...

What would I like to remember about today?

-
-
-

Today I took care of myself by:

Today I am grateful for:

MY DOODLE DIARY

I
CAN
BE
MINDFUL

HAND BREATHING

Use your finger and place it on your opposite hand starting at the base of your thumb.

When you trace your finger upwards, take a **BREATH IN** and when you come down again, you **BREATHE OUT**. You can do this wherever you are if you need to calm down or feel relaxed!

DEAR DIARY

Date: / /

Day:

Choose your weather mood

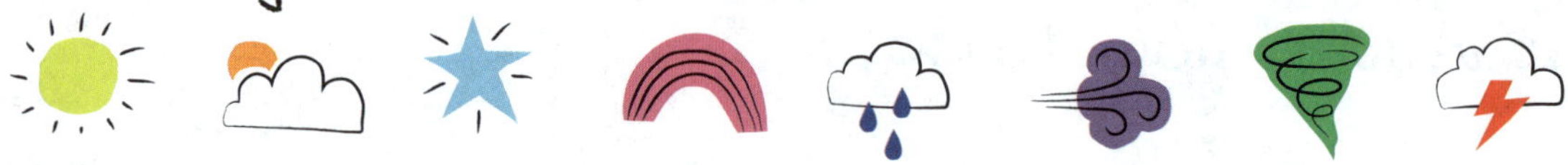

Dear diary...

What would I like to remember about today?

-
-
-

Today I took care of myself by:

Today I am grateful for:

MY DOODLE DIARY

I
CAN
TALK
ABOUT MY
FEELINGS

The Feelings Iceberg

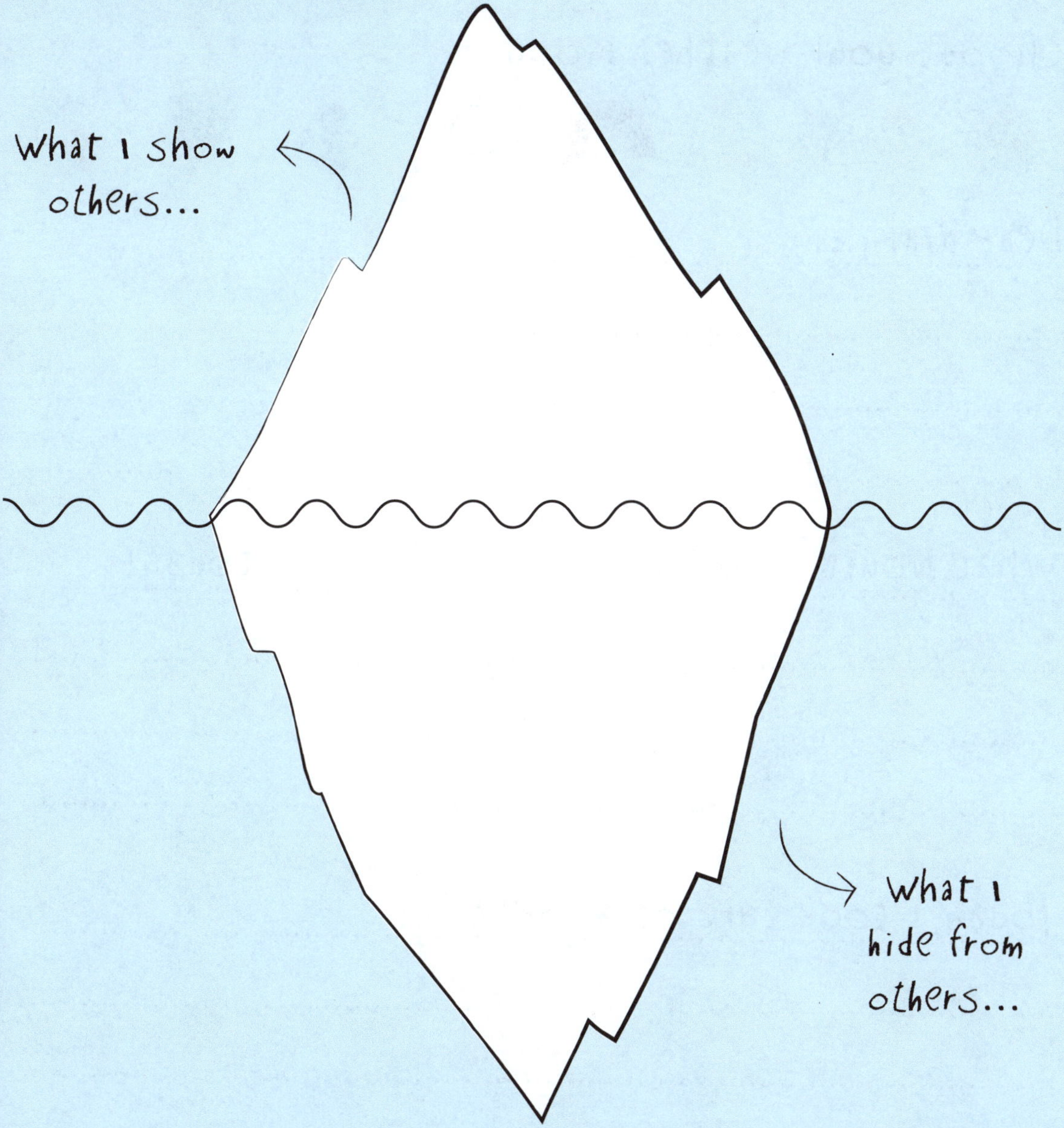

Use this iceberg to write down the feelings that you show above the surface and the feelings you hide under the surface.

DEAR DIARY

Date: / / Day: ____________________

Choose your weather mood

Dear diary...

What would I like to remember about today?

-
-
-

Today I took care of myself by:

Today I am grateful for:

MY DOODLE DIARY

I

CAN

BE

KIND

KINDNESS IS...

Kindness is comforting someone when they feel sad

Kindness is sharing with others, even when you don't feel like it!

Kindness is...

DEAR DIARY

Date: / / Day: ____________

Choose your weather mood

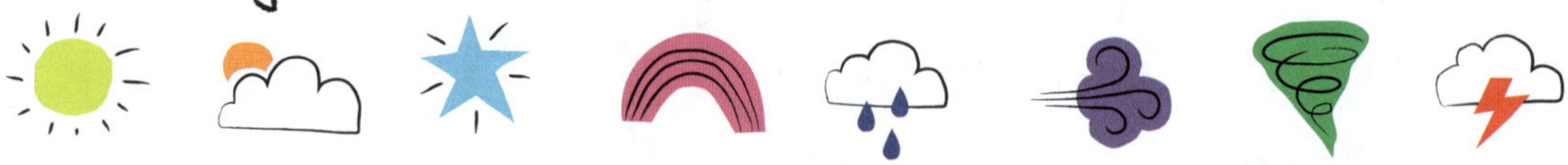

Dear diary...

What would I like to remember about today?

-
-
-

Today I took care of myself by:

Today I am grateful for:

MY DOODLE DIARY

I CAN FIND WAYS TO LOOK AFTER MYSELF

TAKING CARE OF YOURSELF

Self-care is something you may have heard an adult in your life talk about.

All it really means is an activity that makes your mind or body feel better.

Things that make my **MIND** feel better...

+ ....
+ ....
+ ....
+ ....
+ ....

Things that make my **BODY** feel better...

+ ....
+ ....
+ ....
+ ....
+ ....

DEAR DIARY

Date: / / Day: ____________

Choose your weather mood

Dear diary...

....

....

....

What would I like to remember about today?

-
-
-

Today I took care of myself by:

....

....

Today I am grateful for:

....

....

MY DOODLE DIARY

I
LOVE
AND
ACCEPT
MYSELF

SHOW YOURSELF SOME LOVE

Put your hands on the opposite arms and rub up and down. This is called self-soothing and can be a good way to boost your mood if you need to show yourself some love.

DEAR DIARY

Date: / / Day: ____________

Choose your weather mood

Dear diary...

What would I like to remember about today?

-
-
-

Today I took care of myself by:

Today I am grateful for:

MY DOODLE DIARY

PRACTICE
MAKES
PROGRESS

Riding a Bike

We all like to be good at stuff! But how can we be good at something we haven't learnt yet?

Think of it like learning to ride a bike, it takes practice and sometimes we need a little helping hand.

Nobody can do it straight away, but we try and try again. This is called **resilience**.

If we are resilient, we understand that we can't do something yet. But we can choose to keep trying. It's not about perfection, it's about **progress**. That's what really matters!

DEAR DIARY

Date: / / Day: ________________

Choose your weather mood

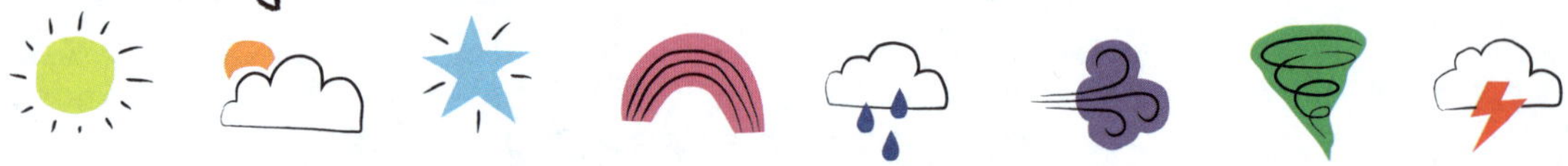

Dear diary...

....

....

....

What would I like to remember about today?

- ....
- ....
- ....

Today I took care of myself by:

....

....

Today I am grateful for:

....

....

MY DOODLE DIARY

I AM A GOOD FRIEND

WHAT IS A GOOD FRIEND?

Write or doodle what a good friend looks like to you...

DEAR DIARY

Date: / / Day: ________________

Choose your weather mood

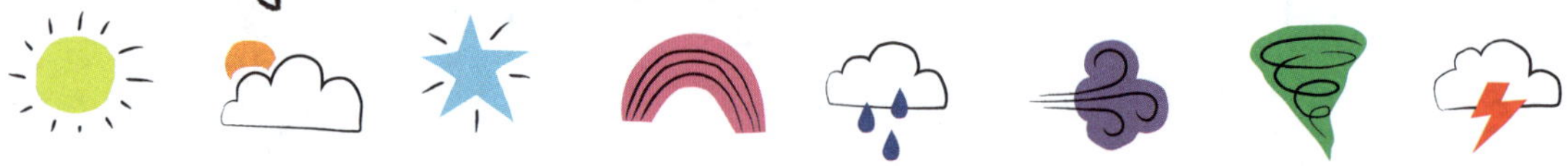

Dear diary...

What would I like to remember about today?

-
-
-

Today I took care of myself by:

Today I am grateful for:

MY DOODLE DIARY

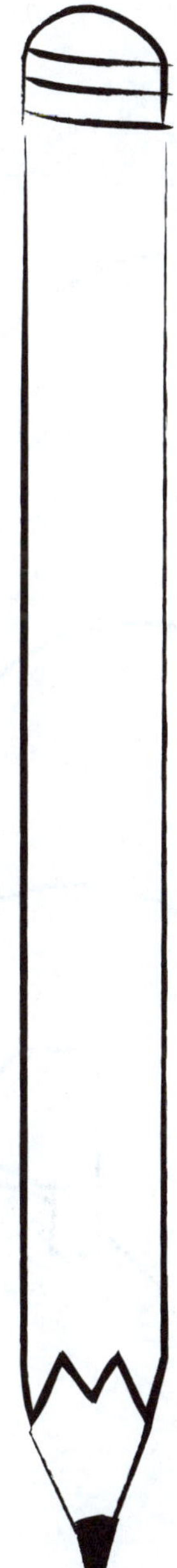

I
RADIATE
POSITIVITY

POSITIVE ME!

Draw a picture of yourself with a positive force field around you...

DEAR DIARY

Date: / /   Day: ____________

Choose your weather mood

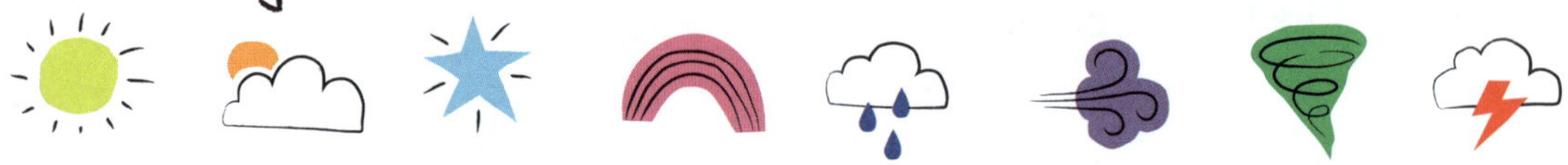

Dear diary...

What would I like to remember about today?

-
-
-

Today I took care of myself by:

Today I am grateful for:

MY DOODLE DIARY

I CAN CONTROL MY ANGER

How Anger Feels

Everyone gets angry from time to time. It's how we cope with it and understand what is making us angry that matters.

Let's talk about how it feels when we are angry.

My face feels...

My chest feels...

My hands feel...

Let's Reflect

What have you learnt from using this Doodle Diary?

What has been your favourite thing?

HAPPY AND CALM

Draw a picture of yourself looking happy and calm and write a few words about what it feels like to be a super-calm warrior.

A CHAPTER FOR ADULTS!

JOURNALING AND RESILIENCE

Congratulations! You and your child are now the proud owners of this fabulous doodle diary! Whether this is your child's first introduction to journaling, or your family's already hooked on it, journaling is great for promoting resilience. As with all life skills, early learning is vital in order for it to quickly become part of the routine and rhythm of our lives.

At The Parent Collaborative, we firmly subscribe to the 'modelling' philosophy - if you, as a carer, journal alongside your child, they are far more likely to do it too. Not only will journaling with your child give you precious time to spend together, but you will all be promoting resilience and practising great self-care.

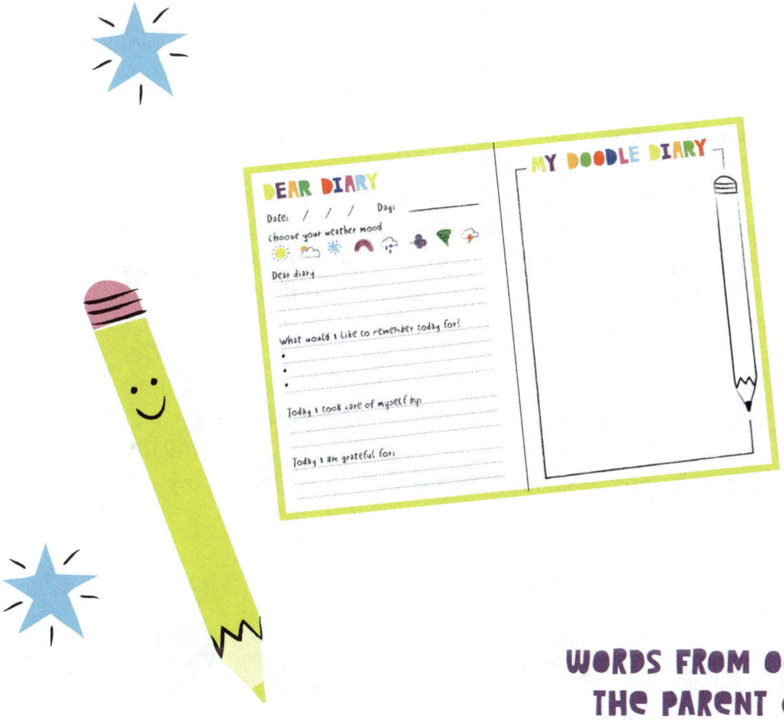

WORDS FROM OUR FRIENDS AT THE PARENT COLLABORATIVE

WHAT DOES RESILIENCE LOOK LIKE IN A CHILD?

It is almost impossible to discuss a topic as wide and varied as resilience in a matter of paragraphs because it will look different for each and every child. Here, though, are some basics.

A resilient child is one who is::

- Self-motivated
- Capable of taking risks
- Able to learn from failure & remain HOPEFUL
- Capable of finding alternative solutions
- Able to manage difficult situations calmly
- Open to new experiences

All very well, but what happens if your child is stressed, worried or scared? Every day is different, and we are all affected by events unique to ourselves and our families. At The Parent Collaborative, we talk about life being a 'moving carpet' – we aim to teach our children how to dance on that moving carpet.

We, as adults, know that things change, that storms pass, and the sun comes out again, but how often do we remind our children of these things? Helping them to understand that, like the bad weather, difficult feelings or challenging events will pass, is one of the first steps towards fostering resilience.

OUR TOP TIPS FOR FOSTERING RESILIENCE

SELF-MOTIVATION

Is your child doing the task they've been set in order to please you/ their teacher or for some other form of extrinsic reward? Children are, by nature, intrinsically motivated. If they are being motivated by an extrinsic reward, you will always need to 'push' them and provide one. How then, can you turn things around so that they are motivated to act intrinsically?

Could 'Please tidy your room, it always looks a mess!' become 'Please could **you** tidy your room so that **you** can easily find your toys tomorrow and then **you'll** have longer to play with them.'? Now they're tidying up for themselves and not just to please you.

CAPACITY FOR RISK TAKING

Do you take control of risk assessment? Consider the act of climbing a tree – a child will only go as far as they feel confident.

If you need to lift them up to the first branch, they aren't ready to climb the tree. If they go and get a box to climb on in order to reach the first branch and they still don't have the strength to pull themselves up and over it, they're getting ready. If they manage to pull themselves up and over the first branch with confidence, they are probably ready to climb the tree alone. You can now help them to set some boundaries – how far should they go? If they fall, what are the consequences? How will they deal with the consequences? No child **wants** to fall out of a tree. Setting boundaries, however, gives them the self-confidence to believe that they can do it, and safely.

ABILITY TO LEARN FROM FAILURE AND REMAIN HOPEFUL

Are we okay with our children failing? We empower them when we praise and support them for trying.

A simple example of this is a child who packs their school bag by themselves, but then leaves it at home. On this occasion, you're unable to go home and get it for them, so they will have to do without it for the day. A child will learn that they can cope without the bag and that what seemed insurmountable was actually ok. When, later that day you chat with your child about how they felt when they realised they'd forgotten the bag compared to how they now feel, they will realise that they were able to work through their emotions – difficult and uncomfortable as they may initially have been - and that they were able to choose how to respond in a crisis.

CAPACITY FOR FINDING ALTERNATIVE SOLUTIONS

If your children are stuck on a project or activity and become stressed because they can't find a solution, do you give them the solution or do you ask them what solutions they've considered? In asking them what they could do, you're enabling them to problem solve. You're empowering them.

If a child is frustrated, acknowledge their frustration at not having an immediate solution and then suggest breaking the task down into stages. Ask them which steps they feel they might find hardest and why. Additionally, think aloud as you problem solve for yourself too, remembering to ask your children for their opinion. Ask open ended questions such as 'What do you think could work?' or at the end of the task, 'What worked and what didn't?' Remember that you are not looking for perfection, so 'What mistake did you make that taught you something today?' is an empowering question to ask. Let them know about the mistakes you make. Explain your solutions. One of our favourite statements is, 'I can't do it yet, but I am hoping that if I keep practising, I will be able to do it soon.'

ABILITY TO MANAGE DIFFICULT SITUATIONS CALMLY

This will change by the day, week and month and is influenced by external circumstances too. We need to help our children to recognise how they are feeling when they're emotional.

'I can see that you're really angry about that, which is no surprise bearing in mind all that you've had to cope with this week' or, 'I really admire you for calming down so quickly, especially when that really got to you. It's not easy when someone you think is a friend lets you down' are statements that will better help them to accept that it's okay not to be okay and that with time and space we can calm down and the world will look better.

OPEN TO NEW EXPERIENCES

This will vary depending on your child's position within the family – the eldest (or only child) will always watch what others do before jumping in, a second (or number 2 if you've got different sexes) will follow someone else's lead and a number 3 will tend to find a whole new way of tackling the experience. Their reaction will also be coloured by how we, ourselves, react to new experiences. Not all adults can rush into a room of people and be ready to party, yet sometimes we expect children to do exactly that.

KEY FEATURES OF THE DOODLE DIARY

DOODLING

The link between the hand and the brain is a powerful and important one. Anything that goes in through muscular memory will be retained much longer than visual or auditory stimulus. If your child is struggling with handwriting, holding any implement be it a pen, crayon or paint-brush will be just as effective in 'training the hand' to write and form letters as any formal letter tracing activity.

It's vital that this journal is seen as 'fun' and a 'hobby' rather than homework! How do you view your own journal? Do you see it as yet another thing to add to your to-do list or do you see it as a self-care treat at the end of the day? Messages we send to our brains form new pathways. If we go to bed focussing only on the negative things that happened during the day, we will wake up ready for battle. If we note even 3 simple but positive things that happened in our day (our cuppa tasted so good, my walk with XXX, the smile from a stranger), we will set ourselves up for a positive day. It is all about growth mindset.

THE MOOD TRACKER & EMOTIONS

So often we see anger as a 'bad emotion'. It's so much more helpful to a child to know it's just another emotion. We all get angry, but it's what we do when we are angry that matters. How can we defuse our anger? What makes us angry? It's really helpful to start by noticing our feelings and then naming them. If we, as adults, do this, our children will follow suit. When was the last time you told your child you were feeling angry or stressed because...

TAPPING INTO OUR BODIES

Noticing where in our bodies we are feeling our emotions is the first step to 'noticing'. Explaining that, as an adult, when you feel stressed 'your shoulders get tense, or you feel sick in your stomach' will help your child do the same.

I CAN FIND POSITIVES IN MYSELF (PAGE 33)

How often do we forget to tell our children when they've done something great? We're not talking the big stuff, like 'Wow! You won that race' or 'You're so kind for sharing with your sibling', we're talking the niggly stuff, like tidying their room without being asked. More often we find ourselves, as parents, repeatedly mentioning the things that didn't get done. As a result, our children are hearing a stream of negatives which can easily lead to them believing they are the 'slow one' or the 'untidy one' or the 'forgetful one'. This page helps them to focus on their strengths. Once you've heard their views, maybe you can help by adding some observations of your own and then you could repeat the process in your own journal with their input.

GROUNDING (PAGE 29)

When your child is having a panic attack or a tantrum, how do you approach it? Do you mirror their behaviour because you're now late, or tired, or stressed too? As adults, we can help by verbally acknowledging that our children are angry or frightened, and that that's okay. We can explain that they've stopped breathing calmly and so their brain is finding it hard to function – taking a breath will help them. Using the 'Calming' wave activity (p.61) or the counting activity (p.64) and talking them through what is happening to their breathing might also help.

LEARNING TO LET GO (PAGE 49)

One of the great ways to get rid of a nightmare is to ask a child to draw the nightmare with as much detail as possible and then help them to talk you through it step by step. We often feel the need to shy away from reliving a nightmare, but drawing it, talking about it and then literally tearing it to pieces is a powerful visual image of letting go. The 'Learning to Let Go' activity will give similar results. If your child finds it hard to visualise the balloon, can you watch some videos of hot air balloons whilst talking them through each of the worries that they're trying to let go?

IT'S ALL CONNECTED (PAGE 57)

We need to remind our children that we can easily 'unlearn information' so that if they feel they're 'stuck' in a negative pattern, they can change that by learning a new method. The 'Resilience' page (p.69) and 'Mistake Master' (p.83) are great ways to help change negative patterns.

None of this is about perfection! We're all human. It's a lifetime not a day.

THE SCIENCE BIT

THE PSYCHOLOGY BEHIND THE BOOK

WRITTEN BY EMMA SVANBERG, CLINICAL PSYCHOLOGIST.

Hello! In amongst the beauty and creativity of this book, there are a LOT of evidence-based techniques and strategies to build resilience, enhance a positive self-image, develop empathy, encourage growth, create intrinsic motivation and instil a sense of calm. Who knew you were holding such a lot in your hands!

The diary pages can help your child to begin identifying and articulating their emotions, which as an adult you will already know is harder than it seems. Emotional literacy is one of the biggest gifts we can give our children – because being able to label and talk about feelings is one of the biggest steps in improving our emotional health. Emotional wellbeing has been shown time and time again to be one of the foundation stones to not just our social relationships, educational attainment and life satisfaction, but even our physical health.

Every day that your child fills in the diary, writing their recollections from the day will help them to lay down their memories and process the feelings of the day.

There are also two exercises each day: a self-care practice and a gratitude practice.

Self-care is something which many adults struggle with, perhaps you recognise that in yourself? But encouraging children to treat themselves with kindness and compassion from an early age can help children to develop soothing techniques which, in turn, can help with emotional regulation. We can think of ourselves as having different emotional 'states', all of which are linked to different brain structures and hormones. Our children live in a world which is full of stressors – raising their adrenaline, sending their brains into fight or flight mode. When you as a carer treat your child with love and affection, it reverses this stress response – switching off fight or flight and filling them with lovely hormones like oxytocin. They can also do this for themselves - by treating themselves with kindness they reduce stress hormones, remove feelings of shame and generally begin to see the world as a safer place.

You may have seen gratitude practices around, because they have become very popular. Gratitude is not about denying difficulty – and the journal has ample space to think about the more difficult feelings too. A consistent gratitude practice, clearly, can shift our focus to those things which feel positive in our life and give us a lovely burst of happy hormones like dopamine, oxytocin and serotonin. But it also heightens our awareness of what those things are and make us more likely to look out for them. So not only does it improve mood in the moment (and there have now been a whole host of studies showing the positive impact of gratitude practices on mental health) but also prosocial behaviour, feelings of connectedness, generosity and empathy longer-term.

Throughout the book your child will also find a wealth of strategies to teach them how to manage their difficult feelings - strategies such as grounding, mindfulness, visualisation, positive self-image and empathy. Not just useful for our children, but us too.

If you would like to read more about any of these ideas you might like to have a look at:

'My Inner Chimp' by Prof Steve Peters
'The Whole Brain Child' by Daniel Siegel
'The Compassionate Mind' (for adults) by Paul Gilbert
'Mindset' by Dr Carol Dweck
'Think Good, Feel Good: A Cognitive Behavioural Therapy Workbook for Children and Young People' by Paul Stallard

EMMA SVANBERG, CLINICAL PSYCHOLOGIST.

OUR COLLABORATORS

YOGADOO

Lucy Stone, author of Find Your WOW, is one of the UK's leading experts on teaching yoga and meditation to children and young people.

After getting into yoga and meditation at University over 20 years ago, Lucy has used both practices to help her physical and mental health throughout her life. And since training as a teacher, loves helping others, young and old feel the benefits too.

Lucy is passionate about normalising the conversation about mental health and well-being from a young age and founded YOGADOO, which provides specialist yoga and meditation teachers to over 60 schools. YOGADOO also works with brands to provide well-being content for events and marketing purposes.

She co-founded The Hive Yoga Studio in Bath, and The Hive Live, its online streaming service.

Lucy recently launched Meditation Rocks – an online meditation channel for children, families and grown-ups.

Lucy is a consultant to BBC Studios, and recently worked on children's yoga episodes for CBeebies show, Hey Duggee.

A former BBC Journalist, Lucy is writing her first book on meditation and gives talks and presentations all over the country on a wide range of subjects including mental health in schools, meditation in a modern world, digital detox and mindfulness for creatives.

Lucy lives in Bath with her son, Freddie and cocker spaniel puppy Barney, she spends as much spare time as possible on a beach and has recently taken up paddle boarding!

You can find Lucy online at
Instagram: @Lucy_yogadoo
@yogadoo
@meditationrocksofficial
@now.lucystone

THE PARENT COLLABORATIVE

The Parent Collaborative came into being in September 2019. It was founded by Reb Grainzevelles and Bella Barron. Whilst first and foremost mothers, Reb and Bella were also Early Years' teachers (with a combined total of 40 years' experience of teaching and senior management), friends and long-time work partners, with experience in the Mental Health arena.

They met as twenty-year-olds. Inspired by their mutual love of children, the Montessori method of education and helped along the way by a large dose of humour, they set up The Oval Montessori Nursery School in South London for 3-5 year olds. Between them, they then went on to set up 3 other schools as well as transforming several, very different Early Years' Settings.

They launched The Parent Collaborative in order to help parents find ways through the maze of parenting young children and beyond. Bella has now moved on to work with parents and children in a different capacity. The Parent Collaborative, however, remains in Bath, still firmly committed to offering support to parents. It does this on an individual and group basis, (in person as well as remotely), alongside Parenting Programmes and Collaborations with the local community, in order to help children and parents maximise each family's unique dynamic.

You can find The Parent Collaborative online at:

Website: www.theparentcollaborative.co.uk
Instagram: @theparentcollaborative
Facebook: @theparentcollaborative
Email: reb@theparentcollaborative.co.uk

EMMA SVANBERG

Emma Svanberg is a Clinical Psychologist working with parents and parents-to-be, supporting them throughout their parenting journey. She is a Doctor of Clinical Psychology which involves a LOT of studying but has learnt the most from the families she has worked with and her own children (who don't hesitate to remind her that she's not a REAL Doctor)

There are lots of different types of psychologists (said 'sy-kol-oh-jist') but the kind Emma is means that she talks to people about the kinds of things that are weighing them down - making them sad, worried, angry or scared - and helps them think about how to put some of those weights down. She also works with some brilliant psychologists called The Psychology Collective, and together they offer support to the whole family. Their hope is that they can help families feel better and enjoy each other and their lives a little more.

Working for so long with different families, Emma often speaks to people about how their own childhood can make it harder for them to be the parents they want to be. Not everyone can, or wants to, see a psychologist, so she recently created an online course called 'Breaking Past Patterns' to help people let go of some of the patterns they learnt from their own childhood and past experiences.

Emma spends a bit too much time on Facebook, supporting parents through her parenting community 'The Village' and talking all things mental health and parenting on Instagram. She also speaks at events and workshops about mental health and wellbeing.

You can find Emma online at:
www.mumologist.com
Instagram @mumologist
Facebook @themumologist
www.facebook.com/groups/visforvillage

REBECCA SKINNER

Graphic Designer

Website: www.supplestudio.com

LinkedIn: rebecca-skinner-59720925

DANIELLE WHITE

Graphic Designer

Instagram: @daniwhitedesign

LinkedIn: daniwhite18

WHAT WE DO AT THE POSITIVE PLANNER

Hi, we're Ali & Finn. Together we're The Positive Planners.

Since 2017, it's been our mission to empower people to make their mental health and wellbeing a priority, and spread positivity around the world!

We do this by creating thoughtfully designed and inspiring planners and journals, aimed at helping you find joy and positivity in your every day while encouraging the practice of self-care, reflection, and gratitude.

We both have lived experience of mental health challenges and understand how lonely and scary this can feel. We used journaling during our own recoveries and were blown away by how much it helped. This experience, along with the fact that we're both stationery lovers, led us to create our original book, The Positive Planner!

We crowdfunded to self-publish our first book, and with the help of hundreds of amazing people supporting us, we were able to bring our vision and mission to life, publishing a number of other planners and journals. This newly published edition marks the next chapter in our publishing journey as we partner with Transworld, a division of Penguin Random House UK.

From our humble beginnings spent juggling this start-up business around full-time jobs and young families, we've grown into an internationally known brand stocked in some of the most incredible businesses and largest retailers in the world. Some of our lowest moments have shaped what's become one of our proudest achievements and we're so happy to be able to share it with you.

You can find us online at:

Instagram @the_positive_planner
Facebook @thepositiveplanner
Website www.thepositiveplanners.com

WITH THANKS TO...

OUR EXPERTS

Our passion for children's mental health has led us to connect with a remarkable group of like-minded individuals that we are honoured to feature in this book.

The work they do in the field of children's and family mental health is so inspiring to us and it is heartwarming to watch them making real change in this world.

All children deserve the best start in life, both physically and mentally, and we are privileged to have worked on this book with real trailblazers in this field.

Reb, Bella, Lucy and Emma, thank you for being a part of this very special book and for the ongoing work you are doing to make the world a better place for our children.

OUR DESIGNERS

Huge thanks go to our designers Rebecca Skinner and Danielle White. Your ability to bring our ideas and sketches to life never ceases to amaze us! You have both been an absolute dream to work with.

OUR PUBLISHERS

We crowdfunded to self-publish our first book and, with the support of hundreds of wonderful people, brought our vision to life—publishing a series of planners and journals along the way. This new edition marks the start of our next chapter, and we're delighted to be working with Transworld, a division of Penguin Random House. Thank you for your belief, passion, and excitement in our work, which allow us to keep spreading positivity far and wide.

THE REST OF THE RANGE

If you've enjoyed The Positive Doodle Diary, you'll probably love the rest of the range too! Here's a peek at our other best sellers.

THE POSITIVE PLANNER

The Positive Planner is our original guided 12-week journal, created to lift your mood, organise your mind, and add a little support and joy to each day. Inside you'll find gentle daily prompts, uplifting mindfulness activities, and simple tools to help you feel organised, in control, and more at ease. More than just a planner, it's your daily companion—encouraging gratitude, nurturing self-care, and helping you cultivate a lasting sense of happiness.

THE POSITIVE WELLNESS JOURNAL

Wellbeing is about caring for our whole selves. The Positive Wellness Journal is a 12-week guided journal with dedicated chapters for Mind, Body and Soul. Inside, you'll find expert tips, simple self-care tools, yoga sequences, breathing exercises, art therapy activities, and space to reflect. It's here to help you deepen your wellbeing practices, boost happiness, and invite more calm into your life—a space to slow down, check in, and take meaningful steps towards the life you want.

THE POSITIVE STUDENT PLANNER

The ups and downs of student life can be tough, and that's why we created The Positive Student Planner. Designed with students and for students, in collaboration with award-winning GP and young people's mental health expert Dr Dominique Thompson, it's more than just a diary—it's a wellbeing companion. Inside you'll find daily journaling prompts, organisation tools, mindful exercises, and evidence-based strategies to help students stay on top of their studies, manage stress, and build resilience. It's also a space for self-discovery that encourages reflection, self-awareness, and a deeper understanding of what makes them thrive. A thoughtful way to support balance, confidence, and wellbeing throughout the student years.

DOODLE SPACE

TRANSWORLD PUBLISHERS

UK | USA | Canada | Ireland | Australia
India | New Zealand | South Africa

Transworld is part of the Penguin Random House group of companies
whose addresses can be found at global.penguinrandomhouse.com.

Penguin Random House UK, One Embassy Gardens, 8 Viaduct Gardens, London SW11 7BW
Penguin Random House Australia Pty Ltd: 707 Collins Street, Melbourne, VIC 3008
Random House New Zealand: 67 Apollo Drive, Rosedale, Auckland 0632
Penguin Random House US: 1745 Broadway, New York, NY, 10019
Penguin Random House Canada Ltd: 320 Front St West, Suite 1400, Toronto, Ontario, M5V 3B6

penguin.co.uk

Penguin Random House UK

First published in 2020 by Brown Dog Books
This updated edition first published in Great Britain in 2025 by Bantam
an imprint of Transworld Publishers

001

Printed in Italy by LEGO S.p.A

The authorized representative in the EEA is Penguin Random House Ireland,
Morrison Chambers, 32 Nassau Street, Dublin D02 YH68.

A CIP catalogue record for this book is available from the British Library

ISBN: 9780857509833

Penguin Random House is committed to a sustainable future
for our business, our readers and our planet. This book is made
from Forest Stewardship Council® certified paper.

FSC www.fsc.org MIX Paper | Supporting responsible forestry FSC® C018179